Journey through Space with Vaibhavee

Vaibhavee Sahasrabuddhe

BlueRose ONE .com
Stories Matter

First Published in April 2023

ISBN: 978-93-5741-270-4

BLUEROSE PUBLISHERS
www.BlueRoseONE.com
info@bluerosepublishers.com
+91 8882 898 898

Cover Design:
Muskan Sachdeva

Distributed by: BlueRose, Amazon, Flipkart

Dr. Vedprakash Mishra
Pro-Chancellor
Datta Meghe Institute
of Medical Science
(Deemed to be University)

Date : 07.06.2021

FOREWORD

Innovation and creativity is not a monopoly of anyone as the mother repository for the same is 'inquisition' that one harbors and the keenness for fathoming all that is desired to respond to the inquisitive poser with credible including evidence based rationalistic answers. This has been the set hallmark of any and every innovative manifestation of any and every type ever since antiquity.

An inquisition is an intrinsic poser in the form of a three letter word 'Why' and single minded focus for finding an answer to the same. It is for this reason innovation and creativity turns out to be anybody's game. However, in reality what is observable is the cruel sacrifice of inquisition at the altar of required effort and labour for accountably dealing with the same. Age is no bar for this manifestation unique in nature and a legitimate entitlement of one and all.

Vaibhavee is a prodigal child who at a tiny tender age has diligently harbored her inquisition in the domain of Astrosciences and is keenly neck deep involved in it both in terms of analytical depiction and fluent recitation of the same with enviable ease, elegance, accuracy, authenticity and also authoritatively. It is to be seen to be believed such is the inscrutable level of her self-evident intelligence manifesting in a rare blend of incredible creativity heavily disproportionate to her tender age and accruable maturity thereto. It is indeed a divinity that seems to be embodied in her form bringing out as if Goddess Saraswati and Sharada in unison emerge out of her day in and day out.

The present compilation of her unbelievable depictions being brought out in the form of a book is a befitting salutation to her unique talent and creativity which would be not only a diligent recognition of her's but would also stand out as a genuine inspiration for all concerned.

My humble salutation to her parents specially her mother Dr. Anagha who have ventured in nurturing the talented Vaibhavee in an exemplary and emulable manner which also goes to bring out a classical example of meaningful parenting and what it can bring about.

I feel myself not only lucky but privileged as well to pen these lines in recognition of Vaibhavee's extraordinary realm of innovative creativity incomparable in nature with prayers to the Almighty to bless this prodigal child with capacity to harness herself on her chosen path with benchmarks getting set out as a part of natural corollary. My words find themselves at bay to bring out what realistically in intend to pen down, hence I end up only in saluting this prodigal child that Vaibhavee is.

(Dr. Vedprakash Mishra)
Dr. B. C. Roy National Awardee
D.Sc. (Honoris Causa) by Five Universities and D.M.Sc. (Honoris Causa)
Chief Advisor to Hon'ble Chancellor and Krishna Institute of Medical Sciences (Deemed to be University), Karad
Pro-Chancellor, Datta Meghe Institute of Medical Sciences (Deemed to be University), Nagpur
Advisor, Human Ethics Committees Association (HECA), Bangalore
Dean, Academic and Accreditation Board, National Indian Medical Association, New Delhi
Honorary Professor, Indian Medical Association
Honorary Director, Centre for Health Sciences Education Policy and Planning, DMIMS(DU), Nagpur
Former Vice Chancellor, Datta Meghe Institute of Medical Sciences (Deemed University), Nagpur
Former Chairman, Postgraduate Medical Education Committee, Medical Council of India, New Delhi
Former Chairman, Academic Council, Medical Council of India, New Delhi

Dr M S Korde
Retired
Professor of Physics,
Institute of Science,
Nagpur.

PREFACE

"Journey through Space with Vaibhavee", is a book written by a seven year old child, Vaibhavee Sahasrabuddhe. It was my pleasure to go through all the four chapters describing our solar system, stars of the universe, black holes, dark matter and the exoplanets etc.

A thought flashed into my mind:

Twinkle Twinkle little star,
How I wonder what you are!

That little star Vaibhavee has penned down such an exciting story of the universe, is astounding and mind boggling. She has narrated complex astrophysical events in such a simple and humorous language.

I wish best of luck for this little child, may she flourish in life.

Dr M S Korde
Retired Professor of Physics,
Institute of Science,
Nagpur.

Mrs Snehashri Bhoyate
Class Teacher
Bhavan's B P Vidya Mandir
Trimurti Nagar

Blessings.......

Hello All! Every child is unique and I am pretty sure that this statement proves itself an ultimate one. I believe that there is a very sacred and divine bond between between a teacher, rather a facilitator and a pupil which is a tremendous strength for each other. Today is my fortunate day as a facilitator. I could encourage my wonderful child to explore herself abundantly.

She is my young scientist for whom my words are falling short. Kudos to you my shining star, who has taken my suggestion seriously and channelized her energy optimistically, which resulted into a great revolution in the form of a book. Readers can you believe that a tiny girl of just seven years with a deep vision and tireless efforts could pen down her thoughts, views and knowledge.

The way Vaibhavee discovered science of universe is a replica of her curious pondering and imagination. I would urge everyone to please spare your valuable time to adore her efforts and go through her book to celebrate her success.

Every child starts out as a natural born scientist and then we beat it out to them. A few trickle through the system with their wonder, enthusiasm and fantasy for science do wonders.

I believe self expression is a vital part of understanding life and enjoying it to the fullest. Keep it up my child! May you emerge with all the glorious and flying colours and may all the success come to you.

This is for you

You are my bright shining star
Whose journey is so very far,
You are the never ending light
I would love to see you high flight
You are the lightening, the bold thunder
I know you are ready to rock and create many wonders!

Thank you!

Mrs Snehashri Bhoyate

Dr. Anagha Sahasrabuddhe
Asso. Professor
Dept. of Physiology
DMMC, Nagpur

From Mother's Heart

No parent is perfect. We all are experimenting while parenting. Same is true for me. Being a doctor by profession, it's a routine thing for me to do scientific writings but today when I am writing my thoughts on occasion of publishing my little angel's work, my mind is blocked and I am short of words.

It gives me immense pleasure to present my daughter's book "Journey through Space with Vaibhavee", thanks to lockdown! During these past few months when children are stuck up at homes, increase in her screen time was my biggest worry and I didn't have many options as both of us(me and my husband were out) used to be away from home owing to work. One day during casual talk with my daughter, she told me about white holes which I had never heard of before. Even black hole was just another name of a celestial thing for me. I tried to argue with her without any scientific backing, that nothing like this exists. Then on her insistence I checked it on net about its hypothetical existence and I was bowled over. Eventually I realized that she has lot more information about space and she also made her videos on different topics in which she speaks extempore. I forwarded them to her Ist Std class teacher, Mrs Snehashri Bhoyate who encouraged her to write a book.

While writing this book, only the facts which she knows are penned down. I had helped her in spellings, grammar and to a small extent in framing sentences. Some diagrams are conceptualized by Vaibhavee and we got them designed by Mrs Julie Bharbhat. Like cover page. All poems included in this book are vaibhavi's original compositions Many diagrams are hand drawn by Vaibhavee and they are added in inset.She is especially fond of Kaushik's videos on space and a couple of more sites viz. brilliant.org and Kurzgesagt-In a nutshell.

If this inclination has any genetic link I owe it to my late grandfather Mr Vasant Phadke who was a mathematician. Only time will tell whether her interest turns into passion at a later stage.

I am extremely thankful to Honorable Dr Ved Prakash Mishra Sir for agreeing to write a foreword for this small work and Dr Korde, Prof, Physics for verifying and authenticating the content of the manuscript.

As of now I just pray to God to bestow success in all her ventures and shower her with choicest of His blessings!.................

I want to dedicate this book
to my late sister,
Ms Bhargavi Sahasrabuddhe
whom I could never meet. In her loving memory…………..

I want to thank my class teacher,
Mrs Snehashri Bhoyate
for encouraging me to write this book.

Ms Vaibhavee Sahasrabuddhe
Std II, Bhavan's BP Vidya MandirTrimurti Nagar, Nagpur.

Introduction:

Welcome to our Solar System! Let's begin our journey through it. I am sure you will love it. Do you know why it is unique? Because only it has planet with life-Our Earth!

Our solar system lies in Milky Way's Orion Cluster. Like all cosmic bodies it is also governed by four basic forces of the universe: 1.Gravity, 2. Electro-magnetic force, 3. Weak nuclear force and 4. Strong Nuclear Force

.It is whooping 4.5 billion years old and is held together by gravitational force.

Chapter 1

OUR SOLAR SYSTEM

Birth of our Solar System:

Our solar system has a star, Sun in the center and 8 planets revolving around it in different orbits at different speeds. Nothing exactly is known about its birth but scientists have applied what they have seen in other systems to our own star.

So, here goes the story : there was a supermassive star and a nebula (collection of gas clouds and dust) nearby. The star died in supernova explosion, and the nebula collapsed under its gravity, due to the shock waves of supernova since star and the nebula were coming near each other thus a star, our Sun was born from this nebula from interstellar cloud. A new star was born in the universe! It was made up of hydrogen and helium. Since then it is orbiting the center of milky way. Its diameter is 696,340 km!

And still it is one of a medium sized star of the universe.

Later years of Sun

The sun continued to become brighter, shinier and bigger after its birth for millions of years. At the time of birth of the sun, a disk called proto planetary disk was also formed made up of dust, rocks and gases around the sun from which future planets would be born. Since its birth Sun is continuously converting hydrogen to helium and will continue to do so till all its hydrogen is finished. This reaction releases tremendous amount of energy and heat in a nuclear fusion reaction. This will continue for another 5 billion years (the remaining life span of sun).

After its birth Sun continued to heat the proto planetary disk. The gases in the disk near to Sun were taken up by Sun leaving back dust, rocks. Gases in the disk away from the sun remained in the disk itself.

Concept - Vaibhavee, Designed by Julie

Birth of planets

The disk went farther away from the sun and gas giants; Jupiter and Saturn were formed first from the left over gas in the disk. Jupiter was first to born.

There are eight planets in our Solar system of which four are terrestrial (Mercury, Venus, Earth and Mars) and four are Jovian (Jupiter, Saturn, Uranus, Neptune). Out of four Jovian 2 are gas giants (Jupiter and Saturn), and 2 are ice giants (Uranus and Neptune).

Terrestrial planets are small, close to sun, dense, have few or no moons, have rocky surface and no rings.

Jovian planets are made up of gases, mainly hydrogen and helium, they are very big, have many moons and rings.

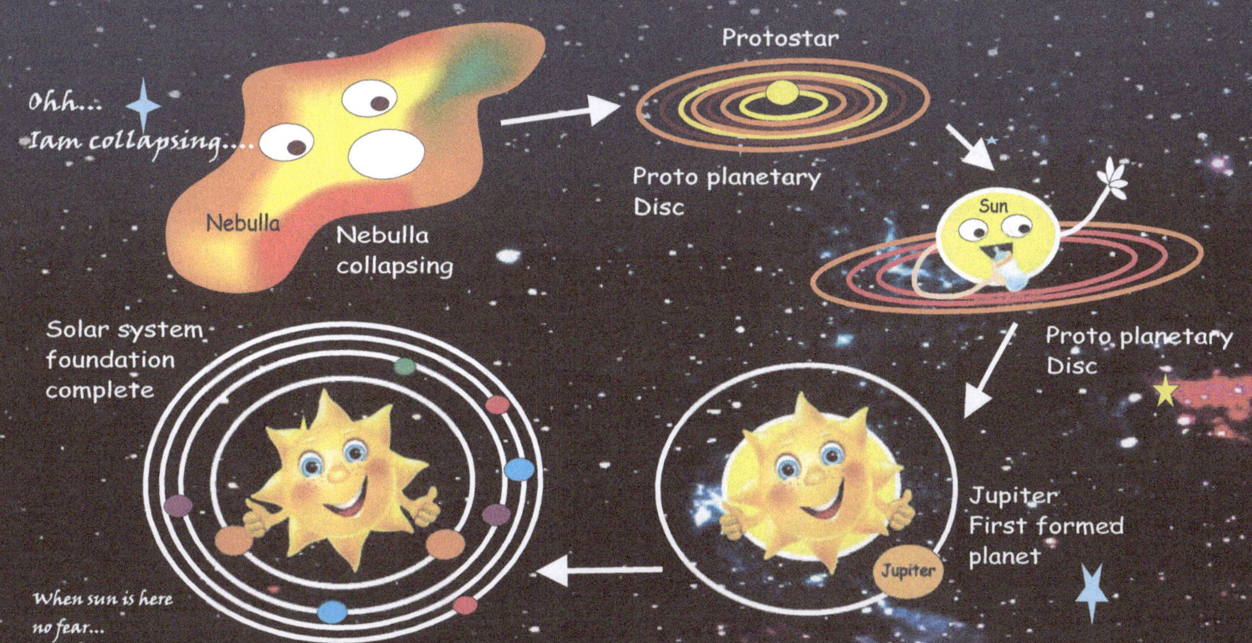

Concept - Vaibhavee, Designed by Julie

Mercury

This planet is smallest and closest to Sun. It is named after the Roman God of heaven. It has thin atmosphere. It is the second hottest planet. Its core has not yet finished cooling. It does not have moon.

Concept - Vaibhavee, Designed by Julie

Venus:

Venus is the hottest and second planet from the Sun. Millions of years ago it was like earth(goldilocks zone) and then something went terribly wrong with it. Scientists think that it was hit by its moon, which slowed its speed of rotation and it started to spin backwards. This impact destroyed its magnetic field, thus exposing it to solar winds, making it hottest. Its thick atmosphere with carbon-di-oxide traps heat (green house effect). Burning lava on its surface, raining sulphuric acid and trapped heat all contribute to convert it into a hell.

Do you know what? Its day is longer than its year!!! Ha Ha Ha

Concept - Vaibhavee, Designed by Julie

Earth

It is the third planet from the Sun. It is the densest planet .It is home for all of us. It is the only planet with liquid water. In fact 2/3rd of earth is covered with oceans. Life first began on earth at least 3.77 billion years ago. It is the only planet with life so far. It is the densest planet of the Solar system. Its core is as hot as Sun's surface!!

Initially it was very hot but after its cooling down was complete it turned into a habitable planet.

Roughly 4.45 billion years ago another exoplanet around half its size, hit it resulting into birth of its sole moon. The current speed of rotation of earth is due to the interaction between their gravitational forces of moon and earth. In absence of moon, earth's axis of rotation will tilt and speed will increase.

Earth' s electromagnetic field, its atmosphere and ozone layer all are protective in nature for life on earth.

Of late, rapid deforestation and increasing pollution, are resulting in global warming posing a threat to earth's atmosphere and ozone layer. It's our duty to protect our home planet from global warming.

Concept - Vaibhavee Designed by Julie

Mars

It is the fourth planet from the Sun and red in colour due as all the rocks and dust on Mars has iron in rust form. It is the last terrestrial planet. It has two moons. Its home to the tallest mountain , Olympis Mons. Its temperature is very cold.

Watched Mangalyaan? Whoala !! Scientists think that it could be the next destination for human race. It also has water in the form of ice. Its gravity is much less than that of earth and size almost half that of earth.

Concept - Vaibhavee Designed by Julie

Jupiter

Jupiter is the largest (nearly 300 times that of earth) and first formed planet of our solar system. It is white and brown in colour. It is made up of hydrogen and helium. Being a gas giant, its density is even less than water and it has NO surface!!!!

It is the fifth planet from the sun and missed out its chance to become a star as it could not ignite nuclear fusion reaction. It is host to furious winds and hurricanes.

As per Roman mythology Jupiter is the God of thunder, lightning and storm. Many asteroids directed towards terrestrial planets hit Jupiter. It has 79 moons!!!

It also has rings but unlike Saturn these rings are very thin to be visualized. It has a big red coloured storm called "the great Red Spot" which is twice big as earth. Initially this spot was thrice as big as earth but it is continuously shrinking in size. It is a hot planet.

Europa , one of the moons of Jupiter is considered to be the most habitable site after earth.

Concept - Vaibhavee, Designed by Julie

Saturn

Saturn is the second largest planet and yellow in colour.

It's density is less than water. So it will float if placed in water. Its made up of hydrogen and helium and has pretty rings. These rings are made up of ice, dust and rock. Because of its strong gravity, it exerts roche limit. It is a certain distance from the planet and anything (asteroid, moon) which cross this limit breaks apart to form rings.

But so sad! Saturn is losing its rings slowly.

The day, Saturday is named after Saturn. At its north pole there is a strange hexagonal storm which is blue in colour. It has 63 moons.

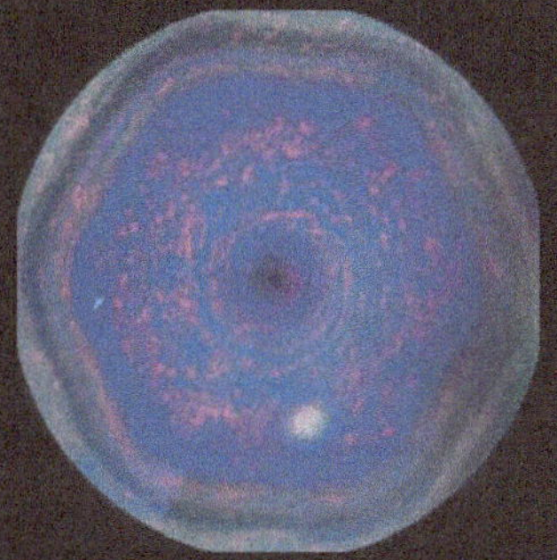

Uranus

It is the seventh planet from the Sun. It's the coldest planet. It is tilted by 98 degrees and spins on its side. It smells like rotten eggs due to lot of hydrogen sulphide. It is made up of methane, ammonia, ice, water and small amounts of helium and hydrogen. It has 27 moons. It is blue in colour due to the presence of methane. Carbon dioxide and hydrogen form hydrocarbon chains in its atmosphere which under high temperature and pressure are converted to diamonds. It rains diamonds on Uranus and Neptune. But these diamonds are very small in size.

It does not have any storms like Jupiter and Saturn. It also has rings but not clearly visible as Saturn.

Concept - Vaibhavee Designed by Julie

Neptune

It's the eighth and the last planet of our solar system. It is the fourth largest planet. It is four times bigger than our earth. It is made up of ammonia, methane, ice, hydrogen, helium and water but inspite of being farthest planet it is not coldest. It is also dark blue in colour due to methane. Initially scientists thought that it was a star as initial telescopes were not as good as now. Its gravity is neither too strong nor too weak. It is the least dense planet. It also has rings like other jovian planets but they are very thin to be seen.

On Neptune it rains diamonds which are very tiny. Under high pressure of its atmosphere, and temperature, carbon fuses to form diamonds in its atmosphere.

It has 13 moons. Its biggest moon is Triton. It had storms called the great dark spot and small dark spot which has now subsided. It also has a storm called cloud scooter.

Concept - Vaibhavee Designed by Julie

Dwarf Planets

Pluto

Till 2006, Pluto was considered to be the planet but in 2006 International Astronomical Union (IAU) revisited its criteria for an object to be called as planet.

1. It should be round
2. It should orbit the Sun.
3. It should clear its neighbourhood which means: the planet should keep its orbit clean. The things around the planet should be thrown away through slingshot by the planet or they should hit the planet due to its gravity.

Pluto fulfills first 2 criteria fails the third one.

Since then Pluto is considered to be a dwarf planet. It has five moons. Charon is the largest one of them.

The other dwarf planets are: Ceres which is between mars and Jupiter, in the asteroid belt then Pluto after that Haumea, Makemake and Eris. They lie in Kuiper belt.

There are five officially recognized dwarf planets in the solar system

But there could be dozens of others that have not yet been formally labeled.

picture courtesy from Google
Source: NASA, Space.com
Image: NASA, ESA, A. Schaller

Astreoid, Asteroid belt, Kuiper Belt, Comets and Meteorides

Asteroids and asteroid belt:

The asteroid belt lies between Mars and Jupiter. It is home to the first dwarf planet Ceres. It is thin. Asteroids are the rocks of space. Some asteroids are small and some are big but not big enough to be classified as dwarf planet. They are irregular in shape. They are made up of silicate, clay. Sometimes they even have a core of gold and contain nickel, iron. Pray you get a gold one in your backyard!!!!

All the asteroids orbit the Sun.

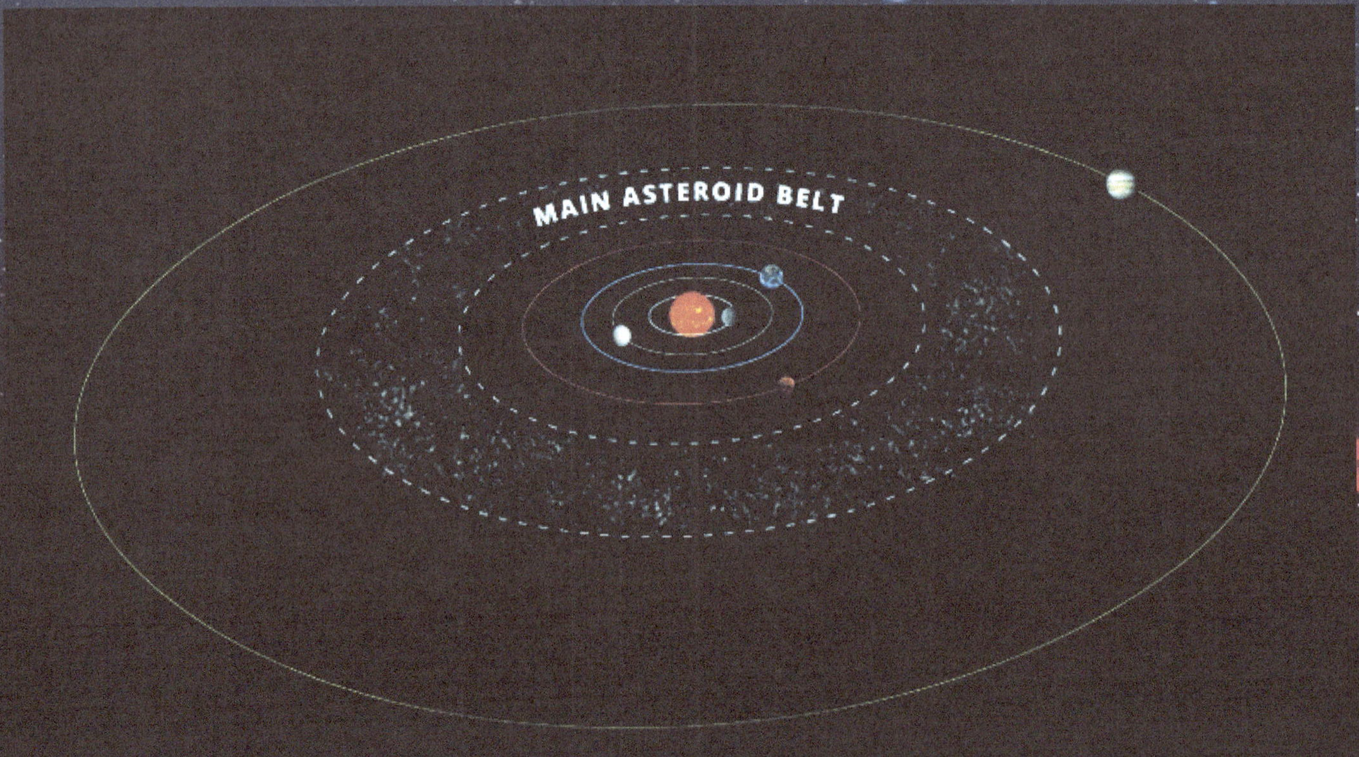

picture courtesy from Google

Kuiper Belt

Kuiper belt is located beyond Neptune's orbit. It is very thick. It is home to the remaining four dwarf planets. It contains pieces of ice and rock, some asteroids and comets. All the objects in Kuiper belt also orbit Sun.All the objects in Kuiper belt other than dwarf planets are called as trans Neptunian objects(TNOs)

Kuiper Belt

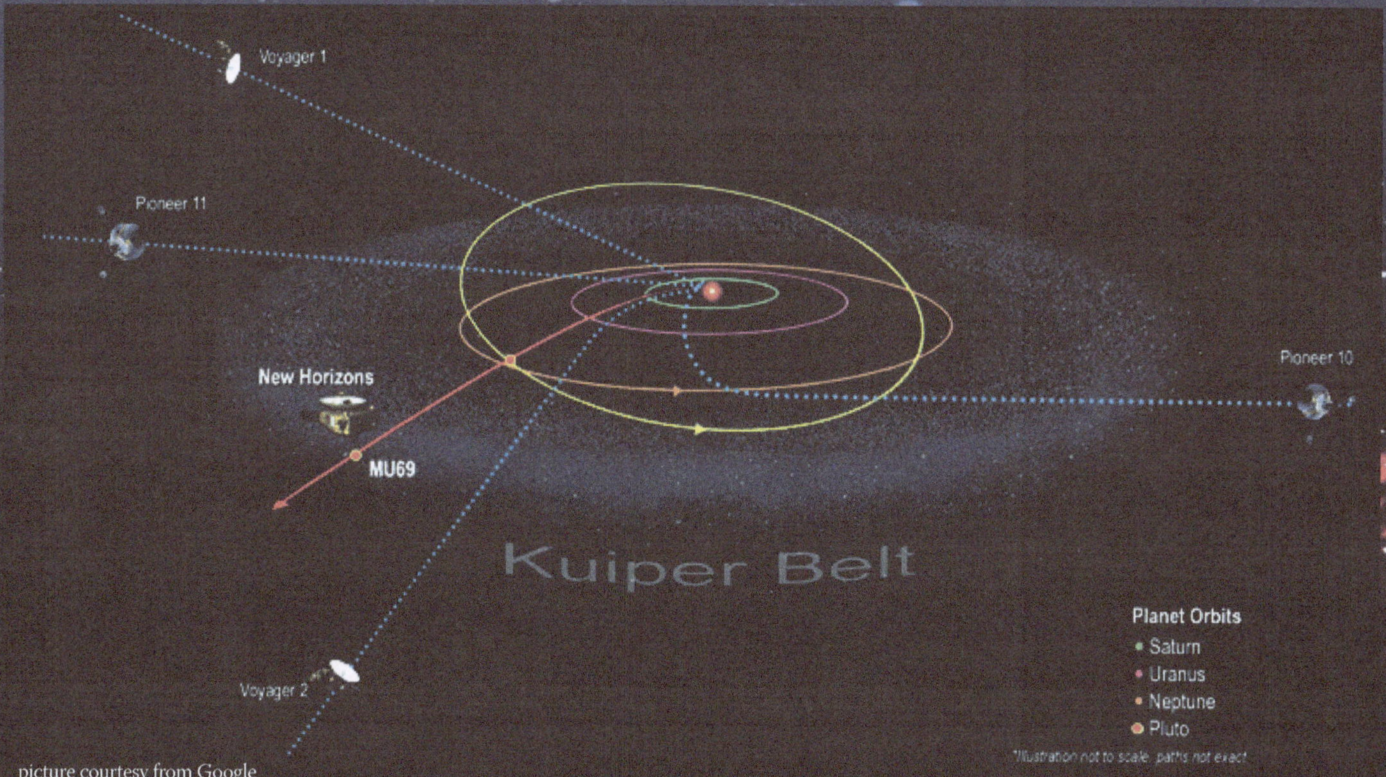

picture courtesy from Google

Comets

They are made up of ice, dust and rock. As they move towards Sun, ice melts on the way.

picture courtesy from Google

Meteorites

They are similar to asteroids but much smaller in size. When any of them hits Earth, they are called meteors and sometimes can be seen in the sky as meteor shower. Meteorites delivered water to earth.

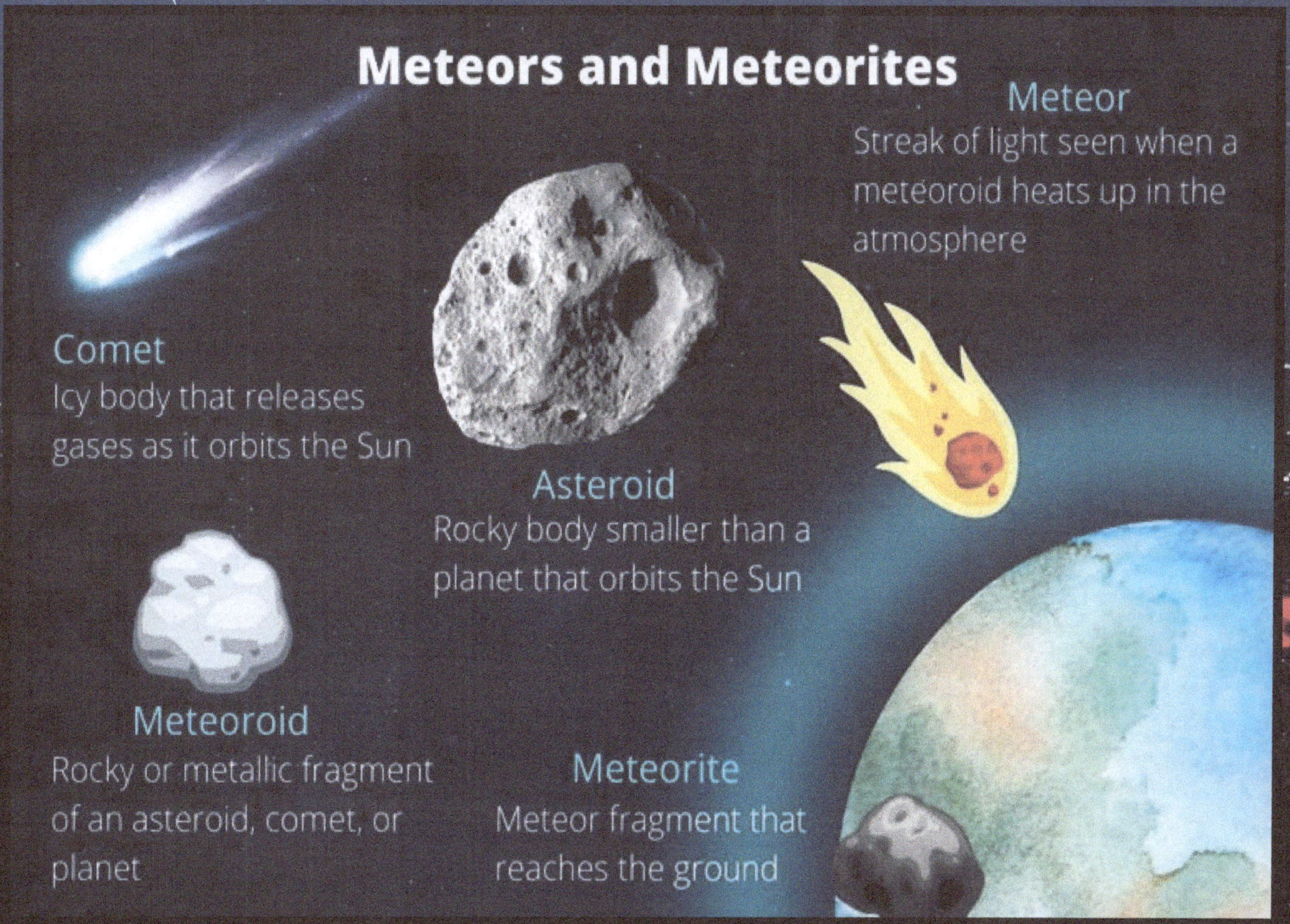

picture courtesy from Google

Oort Cloud

It surrounds the Sun like a ball. It is made up of small planetismals and evaporative material like water, methane, ethane carbon monoxide and hydrogen cyanide. It also has a very small amount of asteroids.

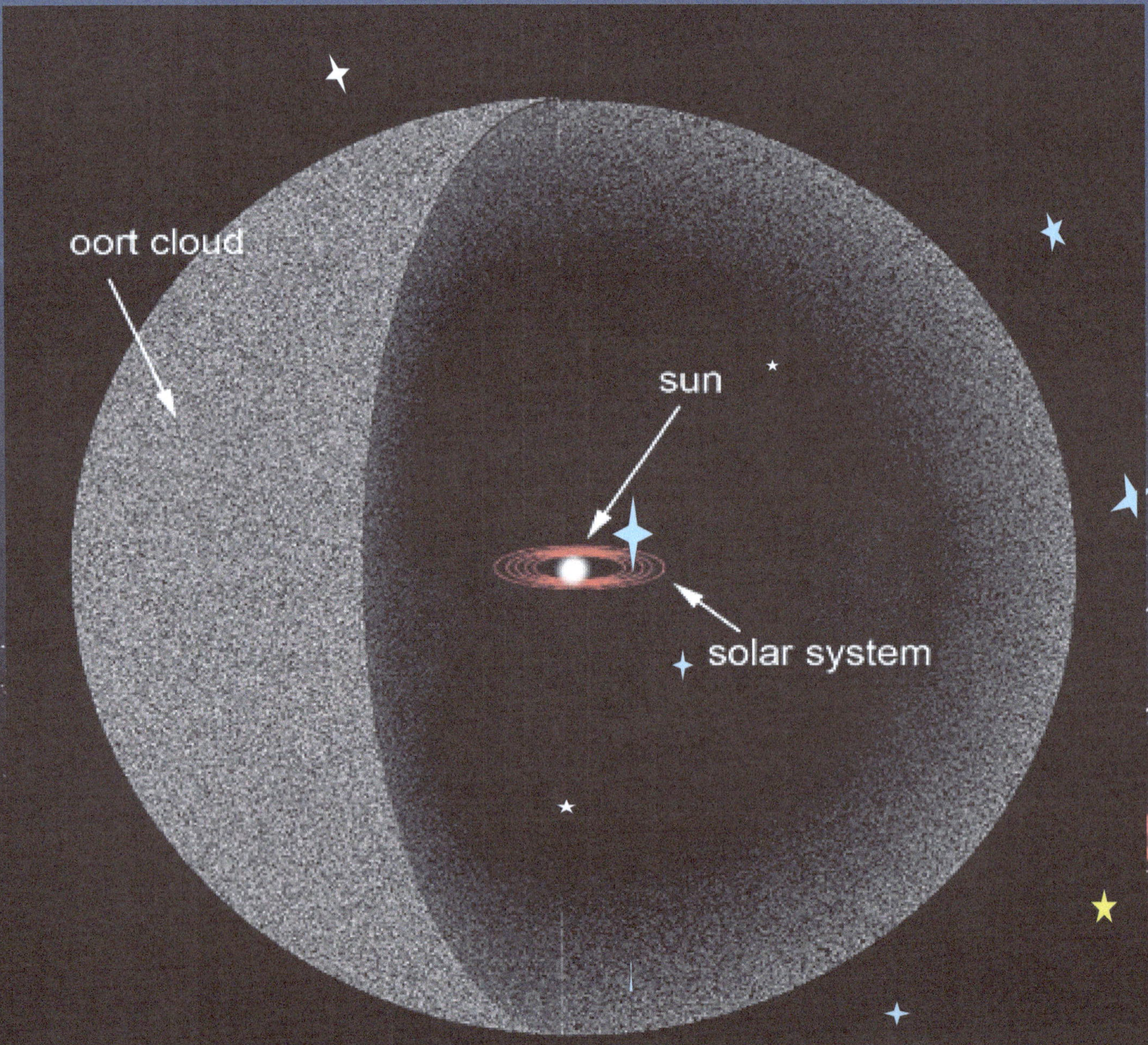

picture courtesy from Google

This is our Solar system
This is our Solar system
With Sun and planets around it!
Mercury is the closest planet,
Venus is the hottest planet
Earth is our home planet
And Mars is the red planet!
Jupiter is the biggest one
Saturn with rings is a pretty planet
Uranus is an ice giant
And Neptune is the farthest planet!
But poor Pluto is not a planet!!
But poor Pluto is not a planet!!

picture courtesy from Google

Chapter 2
Stars of the Universe

Twinkle twinkle little star
Some are big and some are small
Up in the sky you shine at night
But when the day comes our Sun shines bright!!!

In the universe there are more than 700 billion galaxies containing trillions and trillions of stars. The different types of stars are: dwarf stars, giant stars, hyper/supergiant stars. Dwarf stars are much smaller in size than giant and supergiant stars. All stars are made up of hydrogen and helium. Throughout their lifetime they burn their fuel converting hydrogen into helium and liberating tremendous amount of energy in the process. Thus all the stars are very hot and possess strong gravity due to their large mass. Many have their own solar systems. Stars give out flare which are radiations coming out of them.

Smaller the stars larger is their lifespan and they burn slowly.

Dwarf Stars:

The different types of dwarf stars are: brown dwarf, red dwarf, yellow and orange dwarfs and white dwarfs.

Brown dwarfs:

They are the smallest dwarfs and a little bigger than Jupiter. They glow very dimly and that too in patches. There are many brown dwarfs in our galaxy. Their temperatures are not very high. Their mass is not enough to cause much nuclear fusion in their core hence they are called failed stars. They cool down slowly at the end of their life span and when their cooling is complete , they die. When their gas is exhausted, the core remains and if pressure inside the core is very high then the core explodes. They too can bear solar system. These stars don't qualify as G-type main sequencing stars.

picture courtesy from Google

Red Dwarfs:

They are small stars but bigger than brown dwarfs but much smaller than our Sun, only 0.2 soalr mass. They have enough mass to have more nuclear fusion than brown dwarfs hence hotter than brown dwarfs. Their fuel lasts for longer time. They may have their own solar systems. They are longest living stars. Examples of red dwarfs are: Proxima Centauri, Barnard star. Proxima Centauri is the closest star to earth.

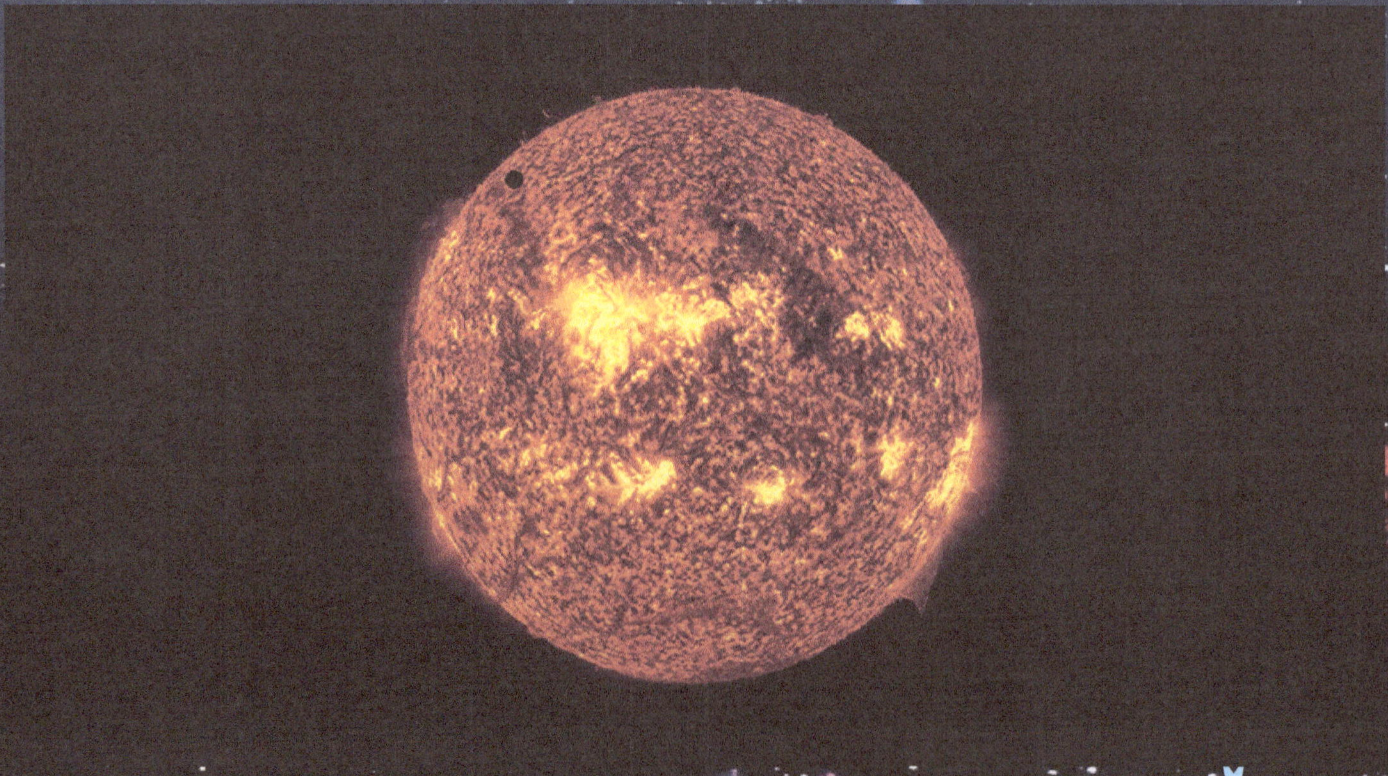

picture courtesy from Google

Proxima Centauri with its flare!!! When red dwarfs die they turn into white dwarfs.

Yellow dwarfs

Yellow dwarfs are medium sized stars neither too big neither too small. Our Sun is a yellow dwarf. Its life is of 10 billion years. It is a main sequence star. When our sun will die become a white dwarf. Examples of yellow dwarf are: Sun, Centauri A, Centauri B. All these stars lie in milky way.

White dwarf.

White dwarfs are the smallest stars. They are hottest among all stars. Many yellow dwarf stars become white dwarfs when they die. They may go supernova. When they die they become black dwarfs.

picture courtesy from Google

Giant and hypergiant stars

Giant stars are the second biggest types of stars. They are bigger than dwarf stars but smaller than hyper/supergiant stars. Hypergiant stars are the biggest ones. Hypergiants and giants die in Supernova, a spectacular event at the end of life of a star. Supernova is an explosion in a big star releasing interstellar clouds with colourful light coming out. If the gravity around the cloud is very high pushing it inward then a new star may form (the way Sun was formed.). The core of such star may either explode or condense and collapse in its gravity to form black holes. A few large stars get converted into Neutron stars when they die.

The life of such large stars is very less as compared with dwarf stars. As they are very big they burn their fuel very fast. Betelgeuse, UY-Scuti and Stephenson 2-18, are red supergiants. Betelgeuse is coming at end of its life in coming few thousands of years(10,000) and will go supernova. Riegel and Sirius are examples of white blue supergiants. Riegel is the brightest star of Orion cluster. The white blue stars are the hottest ones.

Stephenson 2-18 is the largest known star we have ever found. Scientists were surprised to find such a huge star. It lies in milky way.

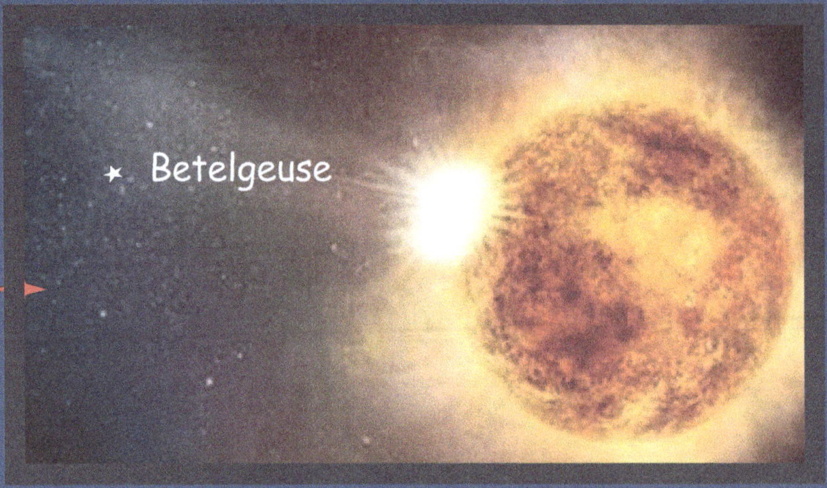

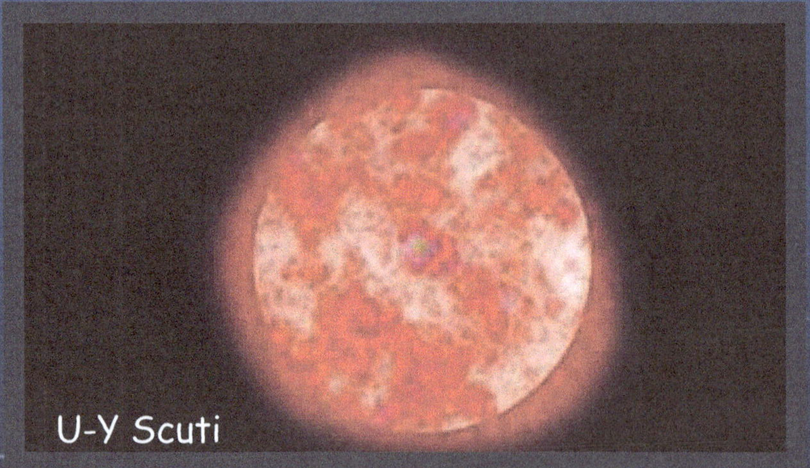

Size comparison of sun with stephenson2-18

picture courtesy from Google

Neutron Stars:

They can be smaller or bigger than Sun. When giant stars die sometimes they form neutron stars. They are made up of neutrons. Huge stars at the end of their life not dense enough to become black holes, collapse under their gravity when they die. Under such high pressures protons and electrons fuse to form neutrons. Once a neutron star is born it just continues to go cooler and cooler. They may have planets but scientists have not yet discovered any planet around neutron star.

Pulsars are the core of some neutron stars which spin very rapidly.

picture courtesy from Google

Chapter 3
Black holes, White Holes and Wormholes

Concept - Vaibhavee , Designed by Julie

Black holes:

Black holes are the most dangerous and the most mysterious things too! As the name suggests they are black hence can't be seen. Scientists knew about their existence since long but they found proof of their existence in 2019. For the first time Hubble telescope captured the image of black hole, a direct proof of their existence!!

There are four types of black holes: stellar, massive, supermassive and miniature. All galaxies have a supermassive black hole in their center. Even Milky way galaxy has one such supremassive blackhole in its center. In addition all galaxies have many stellar blackholes.
Black hole is a hole that sucks up everything that comes near it. It is like a hungry monster gobbling up everything around with unending appetite.
We cannot see blackholes. Only its accretion disc is visible to us. Why?
Space-time and light bend around black holes. Whatever enters black hole nothing can come out. Not even light!!! Even light cannot escape black holes. Hence its direct image cannot be captured. However, radiation can escape out of black holes.

Many black holes are formed when massive stars die and collapse into their gravity resulting in formation of black holes where gravity is so strong that even light is sucked up in it. Scientists don't know yet how supermassive blackholes which lie in the center of each galaxy are formed. They are millions of times as massive as Sun.

Supermassive black hole

picture courtesy from Google

Stellar black hole

picture courtesy from Google

Accretion Disc:

Accretion disc is the glowing disc around black holes. It is made up of debris and material which spins around black holes. It is the material which is outside the event horizon and has not entered black hole.

Event Horizon:

It is the outer border of black holes. It marks the boundry of **NO RETURN!!!** Anything that crosses event horizon, gets sucked up in black hole. Even massive stars which cross event horizon are sucked up inside black holes.

picture courtesy from Google

Inside black holes:

What is inside a black hole can only be imagined, as no signals can escape and come out of black hole. Nothing can survive inside. It is an area of extreme gravity where the matter or light or whatever has entered spins and moves towards the core of black hole. Light bends due to strong gravity and time slows down. If someone manages to come out of black hole the time in the outside universe will be much ahead.

You need to have speed greater than light to escape black holes!!!

Spagettification: When we try to get inside the black hole, we will be stretched paper thin like spaghetti due to extreme gravity inside.

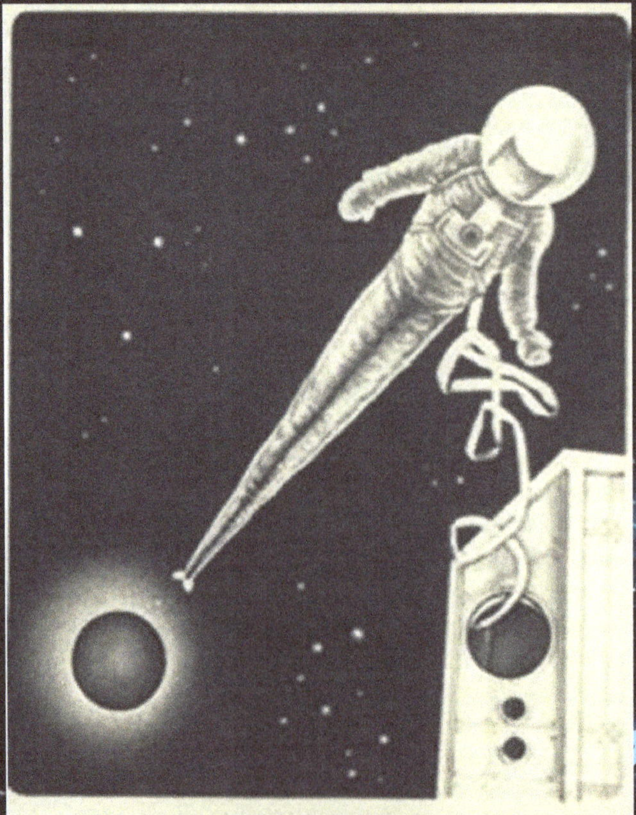

The tidal effect

picture courtesy from Google

What lies in the core of black holes?

Some say its singularity with extreme gravity, others say it may open into another universe with reverse time, or some feel its other end is a white hole. No one knows what is inside!! Some scientists even believe that big bang originated in black hole. NASA could capture image of star of the size of Sun being ripped apart and swallowed up by black hole.

Black holes:

"Black holes, black holes don't eat us
Tell your mysteries to us"
"I won't, I won't tell you my mysteries
I will eat, I will eat stars you can see"

White holes

White holes are reverse versions of black holes. As black holes suck up everything, white holes throw things away from them. Nothing can enter white holes and nothing can escape black holes. Black holes have very strong gravity and white holes lack gravity. Scientists believe about their existence but could not get any evidence as of now.

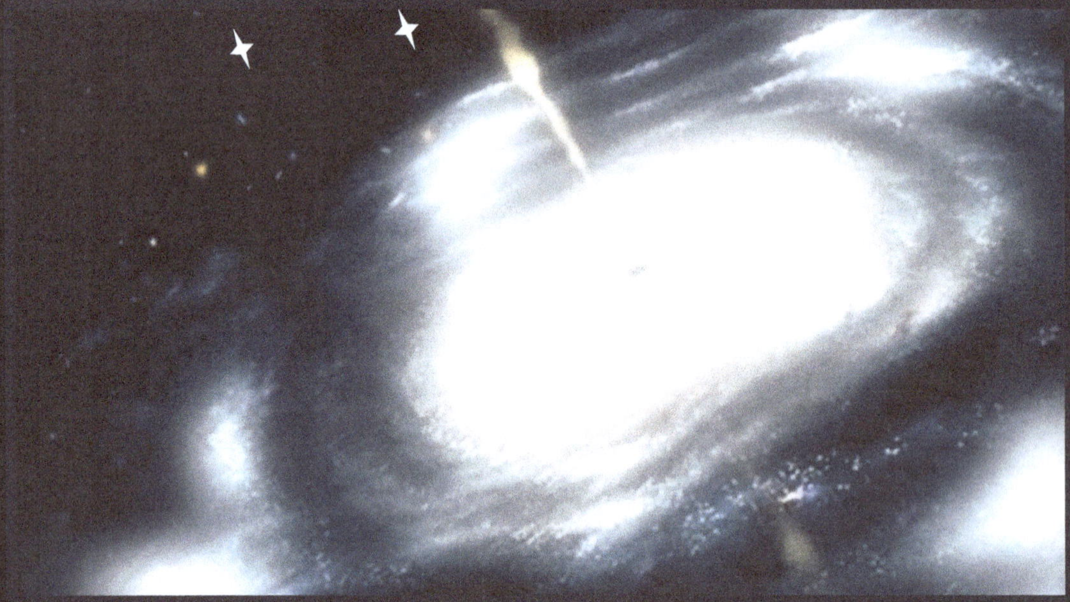

picture courtesy from Google

Worm Holes:

Worm holes are like openings which connect distant space time points in the universe. There is no evidence of their existence yet. They can act as shortcuts to travel into universe as it reduces the distance to be travelled in space to a great extent. If they are discovered travel through space will be possible!!!!

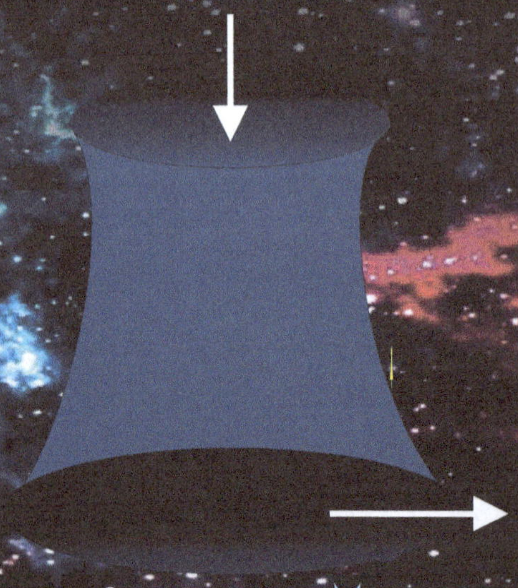

Chapter 4

Fun facts and Mysterious Universe

This is our universe
Big galaxies and small ones!
It is very funny and mysterious,
Governed by its laws that's obvious!!

1. Big Bang:

Big Bang is the origin of the universe. From a small very dense bubble with strong gravity where all the matter was concentrated whole universe was formed as a result of explosion of the bubble in fraction of a second. Before formation of the universe/ Big Bang there was no space/Time!!! Then what was there????

Do you know? Since its birth universe is expanding . It is still continuing to expand .

2. Dark Energy and dark Matter:

Universe is expanding due to dark energy and dark matter. It is the force which counterbalances gravity allowing universe to expand. Scientists don't know what it is made up of? They are trying to find out various ways to detect dark matter and dark energy.

Dark matter makes up 27% of the universe and dark energy 68%. All the galaxies, stars, planets, asteroids comets etc make up only 5%. It works opposite to gravity. Since it is dark, it cannot be detected by any technology

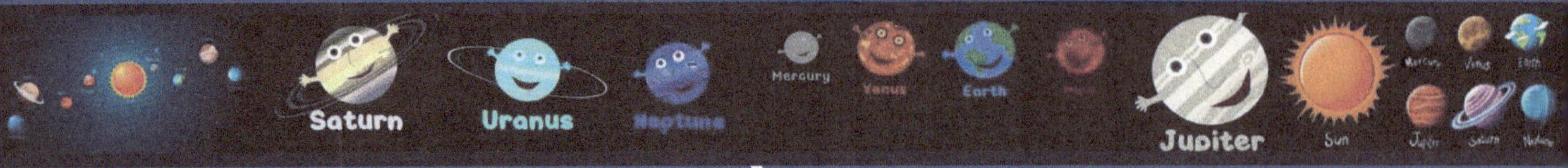

3.Shape and Size of Universe:

Scientists now know that universe is finite. Initially they thought that it was infinite. What they don't know is what is its shape? It could be spherical, flat or open at both ends. It depends on the density of the universe which we don't know!!

4. Presence of multiple universes?

How is it to imagine there are multiples of you and me? Can there be multiple universes? Simple answer is Don't know!! Some think that at the other end of black hole there could be another universe!!

5. Andromeda galaxy and Milky way galaxy are coming closer. And one day they will merge!!

6. How do galaxies end?

They disappear by evaporation.

7. Time Travel:

We can go thousands of years backwards, witness origin of solar system, or go thousands of years forwards and see the future!!! Finally we can find out answer to age old question chicken first or egg???Fascinating, Isnt it ? This is possible if we can invent time machine!!! But sorry its only hypothetical!! You need to travel greater than speed of light to do time travel.

8.Quarks, Strange quarks and strange matter:

What are quarks? Anything, any matter that you see around is made up of atoms which in turn are made up of elementary particles, electrons, protons and neutrons. Let's see now what are normal quarks. Normal quarks are present in normal matter. Atoms contain protons and neutrons in their nuclei. They in turn are made up of normal quark particles/ normal quarks which are bound together tightly.

Strange quarks, strange matter: When you apply pressure to them they bind more firmly. But what if you apply tremendous pressure?they split apart disrupting protons and neutrons and the matter no longer remains bunch of atoms but now a bunch of abnormal quarks called strange quarks. Where are these strange quarks present? Neutron stars are the densest stars in the universe. The core of some of these neutron stars is subjected to so much pressure that it gets converted to a core made up of quarks. They are then called as quark stars. Some of the quarks in them become strange quarks. These strange quarks are very strong, very dense, very stable and indestructible. These are now called as strangelets. If the pressure in the core of these stars exceeds binding capacity, these strangelets are set free. Strangelets form strange matter. Which is the scariest thing of the universe? If your answer is black holes, hold on! Its strange matter!!! Anything that comes in contact with strange matter gets converted into strange matter itself! So strange isn't it?

Thus it can convert big stars, planets or practically anything into strange matter which do not follow the rules of normal matter. The only way to get rid of these is to dump it in black holes. Good news!! No such matter is going to come near our solar system for billions of years to come! Ha what a relief!

9.Exoplanets:

Planets outside our solar system are called as exoplanets. Lets see some weird facts about a few weird exoplanets!

- Wasp-12 B is an exoplanet which is of the shape of a Drop! It is very close to its star and due to the pull by its star its shape has become like a drop!

- Planet inside its star!! There is one exoplanet which is orbiting its star. So whats different? It lies inside its star!! Ha Ha Ha Ha. It has not disappeared even though it is inside its star!
- Nightmare Planet: HD-189733 This planet is dark blue. But don't think you can live there! It rains glass continuously on this planet. It is closer to star, it is hotter than venus and is a gas giant. Hence it is called as nightmare planet!

- J 1407 b: This planet is larger than Jupiter and its rings extend 89 million km!! OMG! That is why it is called as "Lord of Rings". Scientists don't know whether it is a gas giant or a ball of rock or a brown dwarf.
- There is an exoplanet which is covered with water completely, because the core of this planet is made up of ice even if it has water, there is no land to live upon.
- There is one exoplanet which is larger than earth. What is great about is that 1/3rd of this planet has diamonds! If all those diamonds are combined its size will be greater than earth.

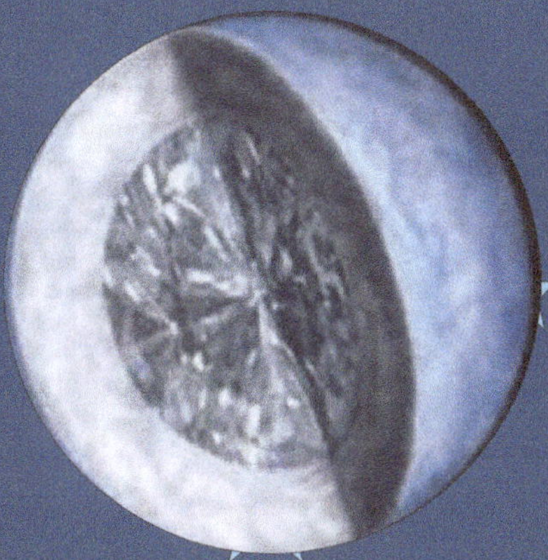

picture courtesy from Google

10. Vampire stars:

There are some stars which consume materials of larger stars! For this both stars should lie close. Smaller star sucks the larger one. Funny isn't it?

11. Restaurant in space:

Restaurant in outer space is set to open soon!!

12. Looking at distant galaxies!

Looking at galaxies is a pleasure. But the funnier fact is when we look at galaxies billions of light years away from earth, we are actually looking back in time!! Sort of time travel isn't it? Maybe even thousands of years back!! This is because light coming from such distant galaxies takes thousands of years to reach us.

13. Binary, Trinary and sextuple star systems:

There are some strange star systems which have two, three or even six stars. Is there night on their planets ever??

Binary solar system

picture courtesy from Google

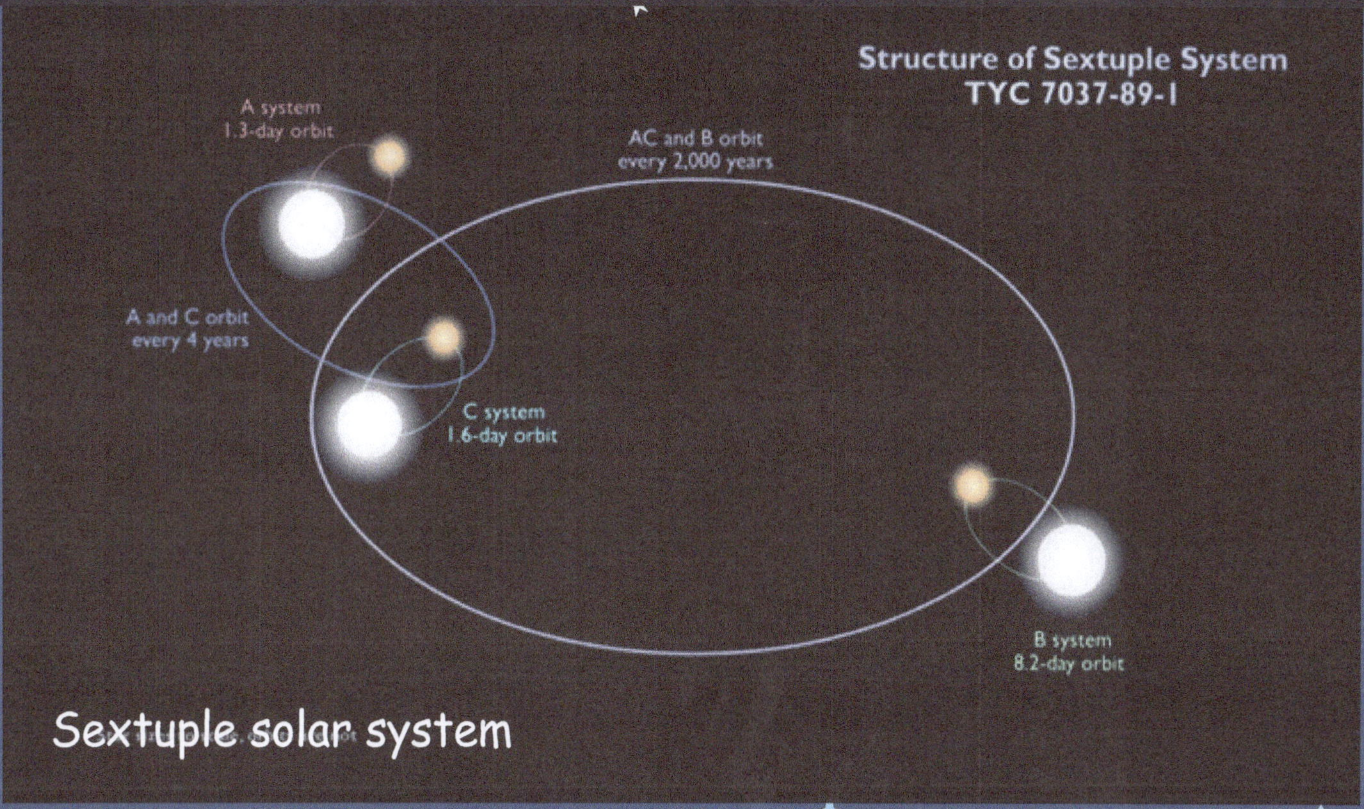

Sextuple solar system

picture courtesy from Google

14. Alien life :

Do alien life exists? No one knows.

15. Can anything travel faster than light?

The answer to this is very simple, "Don't know".

16. Lyka was the first creature

to go for space travel before humans were sent. She was sent on a mission which was not going to bring her back. Tragically Lyka died a very painful death soon after take off as the temperature of her space ship increased tremendously due to some technical problem and its cooling system failed!

So did you love this journey through space with me? For me it was full of fun to be with you. Now I am tired so bye bye. See you soon with another journey.

Disclaimer

The author of this book would like to inform the readers that certain images used in this book may be subject to copyright. Although efforts were made to obtain permission or license to use these images, the author acknowledges that some of the images used may be in violation of copyright laws. The images were used solely for illustrative and educational purposes, and the author does not intend to infringe upon the rights of the copyright holders.

The author encourages readers to obtain proper permissions and licenses before using any copyrighted material, including images, and assumes no liability for any unauthorized use or infringement by the readers of this book. The author also disclaims any responsibility for any damages that may result from the use of the images in this book.

This information is based on scientific knowledge available till 2021. For any scientific updates current correlation required.

9 789357 412704

Printed at Repro India Ltd.